THE EMPEROR'S NEW CLOTHES

A very long time ago, there lived an Emperor who loved new clothes. He wasn't a bit like other Emperors, who spent their days ruling their people or inspecting their soldiers. This Emperor was different! His days were spent trying on fancy new clothes, and admiring himself in one hundred full length mirrors!

Every bedroom in his enormous Palace was filled from floor to ceiling with wardrobes. Every wardrobe was so packed with clothes — not even the tiniest silk handkerchief would fit inside. Upstairs in the Palace was bad enough, but downstairs was even worse.

All the rooms and even the corridors were full of people waiting to see the Emperor. There were tailors, weavers, shoe-makers, dressmakers. Merchants with rolls of velvet and satin. Shopkeepers selling fancy shirts with frilly collars. Not to mention the jewellers! Out of their cases tumbled silver buckles, jewelled belts, sparkling rings and golden chains, each one costing a fortune.

The Emperor couldn't resist anything. He bought the lot. And to make matters worse, he told them all to come back the next day to show him more.

One day, two strangers arrived at the Emperor's Palace, pretending to be weavers, "We must see the Emperor at once," shouted the two rogues all the time trying not to laugh. For they had thought of a very clever plan which could make them very rich indeed. "We must see the Emperor in secret," cried the two rogues, as they strode through the Palace together.

"Clear the room and lock all the doors," the Emperor commanded as the two weavers bowed low in front of him. Excitedly they told the Emperor that they had discovered the secret of weaving magic cloth.

The Emperor looked spellbound. Then the weavers went on to explain, "To a wise and clever man like Your Majesty, the cloth is the finest ever seen — but to a fool it is completely invisible."

The Emperor could hardly believe his ears. He begged the weavers to start work straight away. "Bring your loom to the Palace this very day, and I will give you a bag of gold," the Emperor cried. "I must have a suit made from this magic cloth, then at last I shall be able to find out those around me that are fools."

Later that day the two weavers set up their loom in a room at the Palace. They pretended to work very hard, but of course, the loom was empty. Day after day the rogues spent long hours in front of their loom — doing nothing at all! And every day they asked the Emperor for another bag of gold for payment.

Weeks passed, until the Emperor could wait no longer. "If I go myself, and I cannot see the cloth, the weavers will know I am a fool," thought the Emperor. "But if I send my Prime Minister, then I shall find out for sure if he is a fool."

Now, the Prime Minister was rather old and short-sighted. Try as he may, he could not see even one piece of thread on the loom. "I must be a complete fool," he muttered to himself. However, not wishing to lose his job he scurried off to tell the Emperor what he had found. "Magnificent, exquisite, the finest piece of cloth ever woven," he puffed, quite out of breath.

The Emperor pushed him aside. ''I simply must see for myself.'' He ran through the Palace and burst into the weavers' workroom, and all the people in his court followed him.

When the Emperor saw the empty loom he gasped, and so did everybody else. Not one of them could see a thing! As no-one wished to look a fool, they all waited for the Emperor to speak first.

He walked slowly round and round the loom thinking to himself, ''I can't see a thing. I must be a fool and not fit to be Emperor.''

So, he took a deep breath and faced his whole court. ''It's exquisite, magnificent, quite wonderful!'' he exclaimed. And everyone present, not wishing to appear foolish, congratulated the clever weavers.

"I must have the finest suit made to wear at tomorrow's parade," announced the Emperor. Then he gave the two weavers several more bags of gold, to work all night to finish the invisible suit.

The weavers could hardly believe their good fortune that the Emperor could be such a fool! The clever rogues measured the Emperor and then pretended to cut and sew the invisible cloth. At first light next morning they rushed into the Emperor's bedroom crying, "The wonderful magic suit is finished!"

The Emperor leapt out of bed, and the crafty pair pretended to help him dress in the invisible coat and breeches.

"Splendid! Absolute perfection!" the weavers exclaimed, as they stepped back to admire the Emperor.

Soon the whole court crowded round to see. But as none of them wished to appear fools, they all agreed the suit was truly magnificent. Since early morning, people had been gathering to see the Emperor's new clothes in the parade.

The word had spread quickly, that only the wisest among them could see the suit. So when the Emperor paraded past wearing no clothes at all — not one of them seemed to notice. And as not one of them wished to look a fool they clapped and cheered the Emperor all through the town.

All at once a little boy in the front of the crowd pointed his finger at the Emperor and yelled, "He's got no clothes on!"

A giggle went round the crowd when they realised how stupid they had been. Poor Emperor! His face turned very red, but he held his head up high and paraded slowly back to his Palace. He felt such a fool.

As for the two weavers — they left the Palace rather quickly, just before the parade started — perhaps they couldn't wait to spend all that gold!

RUMPELSTILTSKIN

There was once a poor miller who had a beautiful daughter. He was so proud of her, that he talked about her all day long — to anyone who would listen. ''She is a bride fit for the King himself,'' boasted the miller to his neighbours.

How they all laughed, which made the miller brag even more. ''She can even spin straw into gold!'' the miller shouted at the top of his voice.

Nobody believed him, of course, except one man. He was the King's huntsman who often rode past the mill.

On his return to the Palace, the huntsman told the King about the girl who could spin straw into gold. Now the King loved gold, and when he heard the huntsman's story, he ordered the miller's daughter to be brought before him at once.

The poor girl was horrified when she knew what her father had said. But she was too afraid to tell the King her father had lied.

The King led the trembling girl into a room filled with straw. ''Spin this into gold before sunrise, or you will die,'' ordered the King. And he locked the door behind him.

In the corner of the room was a spinning wheel. The miller's daughter took one look at it and began to weep.

All of a sudden a strange little man jumped down from a tiny window high up in the wall. He took off his cap and bowed very low. "I won't tell you my name," he grinned. "Give me your necklace and I will gladly spin all this straw into gold for you." Straight away he sat down at the spinning wheel and never stopped until every last piece of straw was turned into gold.

In the morning when the King unlocked the door, the whole room was full of gold. The dwarf, of course, was nowhere to be seen.

The King was amazed and delighted with the miller's daughter.

"May I go back home to my father now?" the poor girl begged.

The King shook his head saying, "Rest here and have some food. You have worked all night and must be tired." The miller's daughter dare not disobey the King, so she had to stay.

Now this King was very greedy, and when he saw the pile of gold, he wanted more. So that night, when the miller's daughter woke up, he led her to an even bigger room piled high with straw, and locked her inside.

Once more the girl began to weep, and once more the little man appeared — eager to begin his spinning. This time he asked for her scarf in return for his work. And the girl gladly gave it to him.

In the morning when the King unlocked the door, the room was full of gold yet again. "Spin one more room full of gold tonight," smiled the King, "and I will make you my Queen,"

So that night the girl was locked in the biggest room in the Palace. It was full from floor to ceiling with straw.

Yet again the dwarf appeared. "I have nothing left to give in return for your work," sobbed the miller's daughter. Then the dwarf smiled a wicked smile. "Give me your first child when you are Queen," he laughed. What could the poor girl do but agree?

The dwarf worked hard all night. In the morning his task was done, and the room was packed with gold.

The King kept his promise and married the miller's daughter, and she became his Queen. They were very happy together, especially when a little daughter was born to them.

One day the Queen sat nursing her baby, when the dwarf suddenly appeared before her. "I've come for your first born child," the dwarf cackled, jumping up and down.

The Queen turned pale as she clutched the baby tightly in her arms. She had forgotten all about her promise to the crafty dwarf.

The Queen offered the dwarf jewels, money, anything in the whole Kingdom, but he refused.

However, when she cried so bitterly, he made a bargain with her. "If you can guess my name in three days — you may keep your child."

The Queen stayed awake all night, trying to remember all the names she had ever heard. Everybody in the Palace made long lists of every name they could think of.

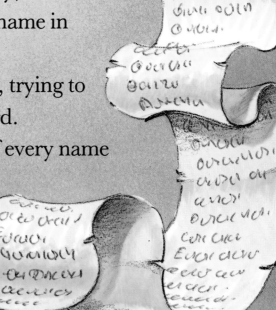

On the first day, the dwarf came back. The Queen told him every name she knew, but after each one the dwarf shouted, "That is not my name!"

That night, the Queen secretly sent her messengers all over the land, to collect new names. When they returned to the palace at first light next day, they had brought back hundreds.

When the dwarf returned for the second time, the Queen read every name her messengers had collected. After every one, the dwarf just laughed and shook his head. Not one of them was right.

By now the Queen was distraught. Only one more day left and everyone had run out of names. Soon the dwarf would take her precious little daughter.

Long before it was light on the third day, a messenger rode into the Palace courtyard demanding to see the Queen.

"I have not been able to find any new names, but I have a very strange tale to tell." He told the Queen how he had passed by a hut hidden deep in the woods. Outside the hut was a fire, round which a strange little man was singing:

"Flames dance, fire shine! Tomorrow, the Queen's child is mine. No more straw to gold I'll spin! For my name is Rumpelstiltskin!"

Can you imagine how happy the Queen was when she heard that name?